STAR WARS™

Galactic

storybook

WRITTEN BY **CALLIOPE GLASS**

ILLUSTRATED BY **KATIE COOK**

DISNEP

LUCASFILM
PRESS

Los Angeles • New York

Printed in China

First Edition, January 2021   10 9 8 7 6 5 4 3 2

Library of Congress Control Number on file

FAC-025393-21046

ISBN 978-1-368-06356-2

Designed by Leigh Zieske

Visit the official *Star Wars* website at: www.starwars.com.

CONTENTS

A JEDI TALE

On the planet Naboo, Jedi Knights Qui-Gon Jinn and Obi-Wan Kenobi were on a mission. The planet had been invaded by battle droids!

The Jedi swung their lightsabers and leapt through the air as the droids fired blasters at them.

Qui-Gon and Obi-Wan escaped, but their spaceship was damaged.
The Jedi traveled to a desert planet called Tatooine for repairs. There they
met a young boy named Anakin Skywalker.

"He is unusually strong in the Force," Qui-Gon said.

He thought Anakin should become a Jedi, too.

Anakin entered a big podrace.

If he won the race, the Jedi could use the prize money to fix their ship.

The boy used his Force sensitivity to steer his podracer. *Zoom! Swish!* He zipped around the course.

And he won!

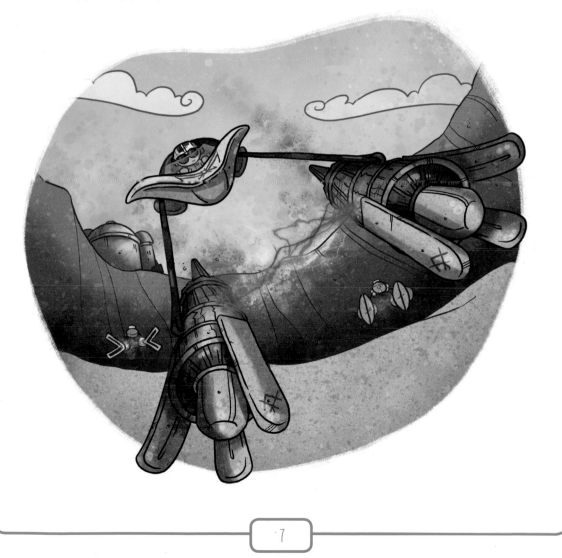

Qui-Gon asked the Jedi Council if he could train Anakin to become a Jedi.

But they saw too much fear in the boy's heart.

"Fear is the path to the dark side," wise Yoda warned.

Anakin was disappointed.

Meanwhile, the invasion of Naboo had gotten worse.

Darth Maul, a dark warrior called a Sith, challenged Qui-Gon and Obi-Wan with his double-bladed red lightsaber.

The Jedi leapt into action!

Sadly, Maul defeated Qui-Gon, but Obi-Wan managed to beat the dangerous Sith.

Anakin joined the battle, too!

He hopped in a starship with the trusty droid R2-D2 and blew up the battle droids' command ship, ending the invasion.

Anakin had saved the day!

The Jedi Council decided Obi-Wan could train him to become a Jedi, after all.

Anakin grew to become a great Jedi.

But an evil Sith named Darth Sidious was secretly trying to wipe out the Jedi.

He trapped Obi-Wan, Anakin, and their friend Padmé with monsters on the planet Geonosis.

But the three friends fought the beasts and escaped.

Anakin continued his training and grew stronger in the Force.

He even defeated the powerful Sith Count Dooku, who worked for the evil Darth Sidious.

Chancellor Palpatine, the leader of the Galactic Senate, encouraged Anakin's growing power.

But Chancellor Palpatine had a dark secret—he was actually the Sith Lord Darth Sidious!

Obi-Wan sensed through the Force that they shouldn't trust Palpatine.

"Anakin, be careful," Obi-Wan warned.

But Anakin didn't listen.

Anakin and Padmé had secretly gotten married.

They were going to have a baby.

But Anakin was afraid something bad might happen to Padmé.

Palpatine used Anakin's fear to turn him to the dark side.

Then he made himself emperor of the whole galaxy!

Obi-Wan tried to save Anakin from the dark side.

But the former Jedi attacked Obi-Wan with his lightsaber!

Obi-Wan escaped to help Padmé, who ended up having not one but *two* babies.

Padmé was heartbroken. She used the last of her strength to name the babies Luke and Leia.

Anakin Skywalker was gone. . . .

He had become Darth Vader, the Emperor's Sith apprentice encased in a suit of scary black armor.

Obi-Wan found safe homes for Luke and Leia, where Vader couldn't find them, and then went into hiding himself.

All hope seemed lost.

But things are not always as they seem.

A NEW ADVENTURE

The evil Emperor and Darth Vader had ruled the galaxy for many years.

But a small group of rebels banded together to fight back.

They needed to destroy the Empire's superweapon, the Death Star.

One brave rebel, Princess Leia, gave the Death Star plans to her trusty droid R2-D2 for safekeeping.

When Darth Vader invaded Leia's ship, R2-D2 and his friend C-3PO fled in an escape pod to the nearby desert planet Tatooine.

R2-D2 set out across the seemingly endless sand dunes. He was looking for someone.

But whom?

C-3PO was nervous. He thought someone was watching them.

And he was right! Small desert scavengers called Jawas had spotted the droids, and soon captured them.

The Jawas sold the two droids to the family of a young man named Luke Skywalker.

As Luke cleaned R2-D2, the little droid projected part of a message from Princess Leia.

"Help me, Obi-Wan Kenobi," she said. "You're my only hope."

Then R2-D2 rolled off to find Obi-Wan, so Luke and C-3PO followed.

When they found Obi-Wan, R2-D2 shared Leia's message. She needed the old Jedi to take the Death Star plans to the rebels.

Obi-Wan wanted Luke to join. He had known Luke's father, a fellow Jedi, and gave the boy his father's old lightsaber.

"You must learn the ways of the Force," he said.

Luke, Obi-Wan, and the droids headed for the local spaceport, but some Imperial stormtroopers stopped them.

They were looking for R2-D2 and C-3PO!

Luke was scared. But Obi-Wan waved his hand.

"These are not the droids you are looking for," he said.

And the stormtroopers let them go!

Obi-Wan and Luke entered a cantina to find a pilot who could take them to the rebels. The cantina was filled with all kinds of aliens! There was even an alien band playing music.

They soon met Han Solo and his furry Wookiee copilot, Chewbacca.

Han agreed to take them on his ship, the *Millennium Falcon*. He told them it was the fastest ship in the galaxy.

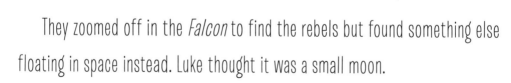

They zoomed off in the *Falcon* to find the rebels but found something else floating in space instead. Luke thought it was a small moon.

"That's no moon," Obi-Wan said.

It was the Death Star.

And it had locked on to their ship with its tractor beam.

They were captured!

Darth Vader had also captured Princess Leia, and she was on board the Death Star.

Obi-Wan disabled the space station's tractor beam so the *Falcon* could escape, while Luke and Han disguised themselves as stormtroopers to rescue Leia.

Real stormtroopers chased them, but the friends hid in a trash compactor. *Yuck!*

Darth Vader stopped Obi-Wan on his way back to the *Falcon*.

"We meet again at last," Vader said.

Obi-Wan ignited his lightsaber and dueled with the dark warrior so his friends could escape.

Vader defeated the old Jedi, but Obi-Wan became one with the Force.

Luke couldn't believe that Obi-Wan was gone. But the rebels needed his help.

Now that they had the plans to the Death Star, they knew just how to destroy it.

Rebel pilots flew into battle! Luke piloted an X-wing starship with R2-D2. Imperial TIE fighters chased them, firing green laser blasts.

Han and Chewie blasted at the TIEs from the *Falcon*.

Then Luke heard Obi-Wan's voice.

Use the Force, Luke.

Letting the Force guide him, Luke fired on the Death Star.

His blast was right on target. The superweapon exploded. *Kaboom!*

Luke and the rebels would keep fighting until the galaxy was free again.

THE BATTLE CONTINUES

Darth Vader and the evil Emperor were determined to defeat the rebels.

The rebels were hiding in a secret base on the ice planet Hoth.

But the Empire sent probe droids throughout the galaxy to locate the hidden base.

Darth Vader knew he would find the rebels soon enough.

And he did!

Vader sent big AT-AT walkers to stomp across the snowy planet and blast the rebel base.

Boom! Boom! Boom!

But the clever rebels used metal cords from their snowspeeders to trip the giant walkers.

"Go for the legs!" Luke Skywalker instructed his fellow pilots.

The rebels escaped Hoth and scattered into space.

Han Solo flew the *Millennium Falcon* into a cave on an asteroid to hide from Imperial ships.

Princess Leia thought it was too dangerous.

"They'd be crazy to follow us, wouldn't they?" Han replied.

Leia had to admit—he had a point!

But it turned out the asteroid cave they were hiding in wasn't a cave at all.

It was the belly of a giant space slug! *Yikes!*

The *Millennium Falcon* zoomed out of the slug's mouth just in time.

Meanwhile, Luke had flown to the swamp planet Dagobah in his X-wing with R2-D2 to train with Jedi Master Yoda.

Luke wanted to be a great Jedi, as his father had been long before.

"Concentrate," Yoda said. "Feel the Force."

Then Yoda told Luke to use the Force to lift his crashed X-wing out of the swamp. But Luke couldn't do it.

"You want the impossible," he told the Jedi Master.

Yoda reached out toward Luke's ship, and the X-wing floated to the surface of the water and up into the air.

Nothing was impossible with the Force.

The Empire was still chasing the *Falcon*. Where could the rebels go?

Then Han had an idea. His friend Lando on Cloud City would hide them!

But Vader got to Lando first and forced him to betray Han.

"No!" Leia shouted as Han was frozen in carbonite.

On Dagobah, Luke sensed that his friends were in trouble.

He left Yoda and raced to Cloud City, where Darth Vader was waiting for him.

Luke and Vader battled with their lightsabers.

The Sith Lord tried to convince Luke to join the dark side.

"I'll never join you!" Luke replied.

"Obi-Wan never told you what happened to your father," said Vader.

"He told me you killed him!" Luke shouted.

"No," Vader replied, reaching out his hand. "*I am your father.*"

Luke couldn't believe it. Vader asked Luke to join him so they could rule the galaxy. Luke would never do that. He let go of the balcony he was clinging to and fell down a long air shaft.

Luke dangled from the base of Cloud City and called out to his friend through the Force.

Leia!

Leia sensed that Luke needed her and raced in the *Falcon* to rescue him.

Together Luke and Leia would find a way to save their friend Han and defeat the Empire once and for all.

AGAINST ALL ODDS

Han Solo was trapped in carbonite in Jabba the Hutt's palace and needed to be rescued.

So Princess Leia disguised herself as a bounty hunter and pretended Chewbacca was her prisoner to get inside the slimy gangster's palace.

She freed Han from the carbonite, but then Jabba captured her and Chewie, too!

Jedi Knight Luke Skywalker arrived to rescue his friends.

But Jabba the Hutt tossed Luke into a pit with a terrifying rancor!

The monster was no match for Luke's Jedi training, though.

Luke defeated the beast. But that just made Jabba even angrier.

Jabba tried to feed Luke and the others to another beast out in the desert called the Sarlacc.

But Luke had a plan.

He had his droid R2-D2 launch his lightsaber up into the air.

Luke caught the weapon and fought off Jabba's guards so they could all escape.

But the rebels were still in trouble.

The Empire was building another Death Star that was even more dangerous than the first superweapon Luke and the rebels had blown up.

To destroy the new Death Star, the rebels needed to disable the space station's energy shield on the forest moon of Endor.

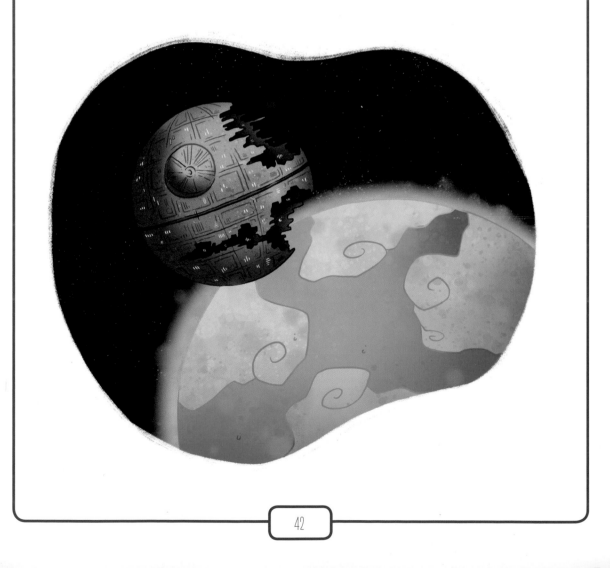

But on Endor, Luke and his friends were captured by furry little warriors called Ewoks.

They thought the golden droid C-3PO was a god!

Luke used the Force to make C-3PO float in the air.

The Ewoks were in awe.

They decided to release the heroes and help them in their fight against the Empire.

The rebels and Ewoks attacked the stormtroopers who guarded the energy shield.

The stormtroopers had powerful blasters.

But the Ewoks were clever. They swarmed the troopers from above and below with rocks, arrows, spears, and traps.

Soon the shield was down!

Rebel ships arrived to attack the new Death Star.

Imperial TIE fighters fired green laser blasts at them, but the rebel pilots refused to give up.

They needed to fly *inside* the Death Star and blast it from within to destroy the superweapon and save the galaxy.

Meanwhile, Luke had a different mission. He believed he could save his father, Darth Vader, from the dark side.

"I know there is good in you," said Luke.

But Darth Vader drew his lightsaber and attacked!

Vader's Sith master—the evil Emperor—wanted Luke to turn to the dark side.

"Give in to your anger," the Emperor told Luke.

When Luke refused, the Sith attacked him with lightning.

Suddenly, Darth Vader picked up the Emperor and threw him down a seemingly bottomless pit!

Luke had been right. There *was* still good in Vader.

Deep down he was still the Jedi hero Anakin Skywalker.

Luke had saved his father from the dark side.

And the rebels had destroyed the Death Star and defeated the Empire.

Down on Endor, Luke celebrated with the Ewoks and his friends-including Leia, who he had learned was his twin sister!

The galaxy was finally free.

NEW HEROES FOR THE GALAXY

On the desert planet Jakku, three new friends named Rey, Finn, and BB-8 were on the run from an evil group called the First Order.

The First Order wanted a map that BB-8 was carrying.

The friends hopped in an old ship called the *Millennium Falcon* and blasted away from Jakku. *Vroooom!*

But the *Falcon* belonged to the rebel heroes Han Solo and Chewbacca!

Han and Chewie agreed to help Rey and Finn get BB-8 back to the Resistance.

The Resistance–led by Han and Chewie's old friend General Leia–was trying to save the galaxy from the First Order.

Han knew his friend Maz Kanata could help them.

They flew the *Falcon* to Maz's castle on the planet Takodana.

Maz was a small alien with big goggles. She gave Rey something very special.

It was a lightsaber that had once belonged to Leia's brother, Luke Skywalker, a famous Jedi Master.

Suddenly, the First Order arrived and started attacking Maz's castle!

They were looking for BB-8.

TIE fighters blasted the castle with green laser fire.

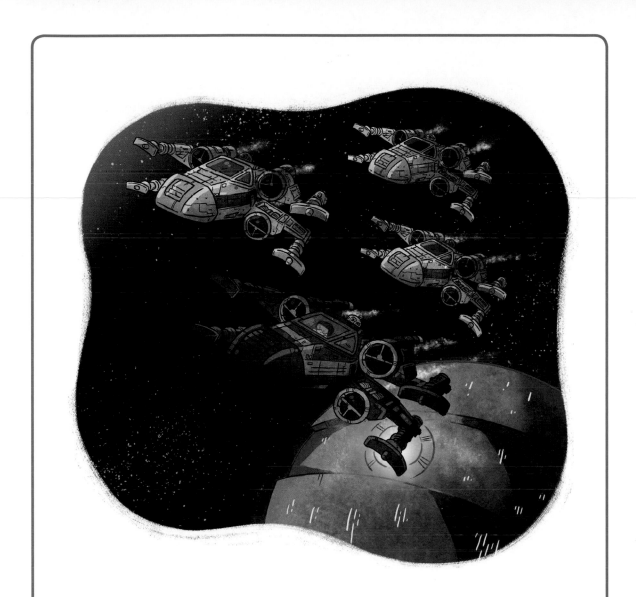

The Resistance needed to fight back.

The First Order had built a deadly superweapon called the Starkiller.

Resistance X-wings flew into battle to destroy the weapon.

Rey joined the fight, too, battling the First Order warrior Kylo Ren with Luke's lightsaber.

Once Han and Leia's son, Ben, he had fallen to the dark side to become Kylo.

"You need a teacher," he told Rey, who was strong in the Force.

But Rey didn't want to join the dark side.

She knocked Kylo to the ground and escaped.

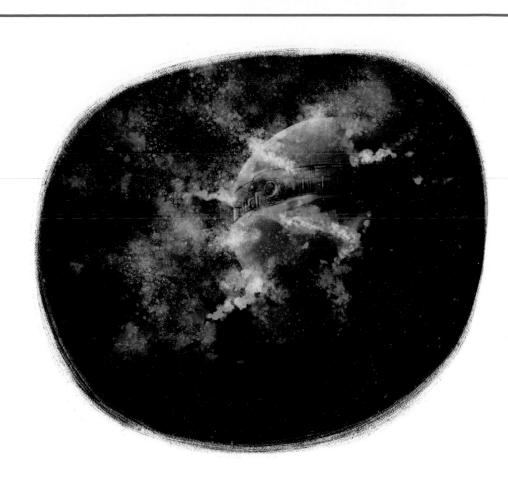

The Resistance managed to destroy the Starkiller. The superweapon exploded in a shower of sparks!

But the First Order was still powerful, and Rey knew she would have to fight Kylo Ren again.

He had been right. Rey *did* need a teacher to show her the ways of the Force.

BB-8's map led to Luke Skywalker.

The First Order had wanted the map so they could defeat Luke—the galaxy's last Jedi.

But Rey used the map to find Luke on the distant planet Ahch-To so she could ask him to teach her the ways of the Force.

Luke didn't want to teach anyone ever again, though . . .

. . . not after Luke's sister, Leia, trusted him to train her son, Ben, who had turned to the dark side to become Kylo Ren.

Rey was stubborn, though. She followed Luke until he agreed to teach her.

But the more Rey learned, the more she believed she could save Kylo from the dark side.

Rey went to find Kylo, but she was captured by the First Order.

Kylo rescued her, and the two fought a band of First Order guards side by side.

Had she saved him from the dark side?

No, Kylo wanted Rey to join *him!*

"We can rule together," he promised her.

Rey refused Kylo's offer and escaped.

She found her friends in the Resistance on the planet Crait-zooming across salt flats in old ski speeders to battle massive First Order AT-M6 walkers.

But the Resistance was outnumbered and soon had to retreat to a cave base nearby.

They were trapped and needed help.

Suddenly, Luke Skywalker appeared!

Kylo Ren insisted on fighting the old Jedi himself.

But no matter how hard or fast Kylo swung his lightsaber, Luke always found a way to dodge the crackling red sword.

Luke was just distracting Kylo long enough for the Resistance to escape.

And escape they did!

Rey used the Force to lift a wall of heavy boulders from the back of the cave base to free her friends.

Luke had never actually been on Crait.

He had used all his strength to project himself from Ahch-To onto Crait through the Force to help the Resistance.

As the Resistance fled from the First Order, Rey turned to General Leia.

"How do we build a rebellion from this?" she asked, looking around at the few fighters who remained.

"We have everything we need," Leia replied with a smile.

And Leia was right.

Because the Resistance had *hope*.

THE FINAL FIGHT

Rey deflected blasts from a training remote with her lightsaber. *Zap!*

The Resistance had learned that the old evil Sith Emperor Palpatine had resurfaced on a planet called Exegol, with a massive fleet of Star Destroyers to help Kylo Ren and the First Order!

Rey would need every bit of her Jedi training to stop them.

Unfortunately, the Resistance didn't know where Exegol *was*.

They needed a Sith wayfinder to guide them to the distant planet. Kylo Ren had one, but they heard there might be a clue to the location of another wayfinder on the desert world Pasaana.

So Rey and her friends set off in the *Millennium Falcon*.

On Pasaana, the heroes dodged First Order troopers on fast speeders and managed to find the clue to the wayfinder they were looking for.

It was written on an old dagger in an ancient Sith language.

The droid C-3PO could read the message, but there was still a problem.

"My programming forbids me from translating it," he said.

Rey and her friends–including the little droid D-O, whom they had met along their journey–found a droidsmith named Babu Frik, who bypassed C-3PO's programming.

The golden droid translated the Sith language to reveal that the wayfinder was in a piece of wreckage from the old Empire's second Death Star in the ocean of Kef Bir.

On Kef Bir, the heroes met a warrior named Jannah, who warned that they would need to wait until the waves died down to travel out to the Death Star wreckage.

Rey knew they didn't have any time to lose, though, so she sailed across the deadly sea by herself to find the wayfinder.

But Kylo Ren was waiting for her there.

Destroying the wayfinder, he urged Rey to join the dark side because the evil Emperor was her grandfather.

The two battled with their lightsabers.

Rey wounded Kylo but then sensed that Leia, his mother and Rey's friend, had become one with the Force.

In shock, Rey healed Kylo with her own life force.

Confused and scared, Rey fled to Ahch-To in Kylo's TIE and set the ship on fire so she couldn't leave.

But Rey's old teacher, Luke Skywalker, appeared to her through the Force.

"Confronting fear is the destiny of a Jedi," he encouraged.

He gave Rey Leia's old lightsaber and raised his X-wing from the sea for her to use.

Rey used Kylo's wayfinder to reach Exegol.

And with its coordinates, the Resistance soon arrived to stop the Emperor's fleet of Star Destroyers.

Ben was there, too. He'd left Kylo and the dark side for good.

Together, Rey and Ben confronted the evil Emperor.

But the Sith used dark power to steal their life force!

The Emperor shot lightning from his hands, but Rey refused to give up.

Using the last of her strength, and the Force, Rey called on every Jedi who had ever lived and deflected the Emperor's lightning with Luke and Leia's lightsabers, destroying the Sith once and for all.

Then Ben used the last of his life force to heal Rey.

The galaxy was finally safe.

Rey traveled to Tatooine, the desert planet where Qui-Gon had met Anakin Skywalker all those years before and where Luke Skywalker had met two droids who had turned his life upside down.

These stories had shaped the galaxy, and Rey would carry them with her, wherever her journey led.